Dear Parent:
Your child's love of reading starts here!

Every child learns to read in a different way and at his or her own speed. Some go back and forth between reading levels and read favorite books again and again. Others read through each level in order. You can help your young reader improve and become more confident by encouraging his or her own interests and abilities. From books your child reads with you to the first books he or she reads alone, there are I Can Read Books for every stage of reading:

SHARED READING
Basic language, word repetition, and whimsical illustrations, ideal for sharing with your emergent reader

BEGINNING READING
Short sentences, familiar words, and simple concepts for children eager to read on their own

READING WITH HELP
Engaging stories, longer sentences, and language play for developing readers

READING ALONE
Complex plots, challenging vocabulary, and high-interest topics for the independent reader

ADVANCED READING
Short paragraphs, chapters, and exciting themes for the perfect bridge to chapter books

I Can Read Books have introduced children to the joy of reading since 1957. Featuring award-winning authors and illustrators and a fabulous cast of beloved characters, I Can Read Books set the standard for beginning readers.

A lifetime of discovery begins with the magical words **"I Can Read!"**

Visit www.icanread.com for information
on enriching your child's reading experience.

Library of Congress Control Number: 2016952349
ISBN 978-0-06-240432-9 (trade bdg.) — ISBN 978-0-06-240431-2 (pbk.)

17 18 19 20 21   LSCC   10 9 8 7 6 5 4 3 2   ❖   First Edition

I Can Read!

SHARED My First READING

Pete the Cat
AND THE TIP-TOP TREE HOUSE
by James Dean

HARPER

An Imprint of HarperCollinsPublishers

Pete the Cat has built a
tree house.

He calls his friends.

"I just built a tree house,"
he says.

"Come over to play."

Pete's friends show up.
"This is great," say his
friends.
"But it is a little small."

"You are right," says Pete.
"It is too small.
I will fix that!"

Pete starts building a bigger
tree house.

"Do you want some help?"
asks Callie.

"Sure," says Pete.

Callie carries up more wood.

"Can I help, too?"
asks Marty.
"Sure!" says Pete.

Together they build a tower
for Pete's tree house.

"Let's have a tree house party," says Marty.

"A party?" says Pete.

"But what will everyone do?"

"I can help with that,"
says Emma.

"This is great!" says Pete.

"Let's do it."

Pete, Marty, Callie, Emma,
and Grumpy Toad get right
to work.

They build an arcade.

They fill it with fun games.

They build a bowling alley.

It has twenty lanes.

They build a wave pool.

Pete can surf indoors!

They build a movie theater

and a skate park

and a climbing wall

and an ice rink.

Pete's friends all come
for the party.

Pete takes one friend
to the bowling alley.

He takes one friend
to the movie theater.

Pete takes one friend
to the skate park.

Pete lets one friend surf
in the wave pool.

"Is everyone here?"
asks Pete.

"Yeah, but we're all alone!"
his friends say.
"We came to play with
each other."

"Oh!" says Pete.
"Everyone meet down
at the jungle gym."

Everyone climbs down.
"This tree house is
amazing," say his friends.

"Thanks," says Pete.

"I'm so glad it brought us all together."